# The Fairy Isle of Coosanure

Best wishes to Sheila !

French

Published by
Wolfhound Press,
68 Mountjoy Square, Dublin 1.

© Frank Egan 1981
Illustrations by Jeanette Dunne
© Wolfhound Press

British Library Cataloguing in Publication Data
    Egan, Frank
        The fairy Isle of Coosanure.
        I. Title
        823'.914 [J] PZ7

ISBN 0-905473-70-1

Design and layout by Jarlath Hayes
Typesetting by Redsetter Ltd.

Printed in the Republic of Ireland
by E. & T. O'Brien Ltd.,
Barrow Street, Dublin.

This book is published with the assistance of
the Arts Council (An Chomhairle Ealaíon)

# The Fairy Isle of Coosanure

## FRANK EGAN

Illustrated by
Jeanette Dunne

WOLFHOUND PRESS

*For my daughters, Ailish and Emer, whose innocence was the inspiration for these stories, for their little friends, Therese and Margaret, who were such good listeners, and for my wife, Maureen, who was the real fairy-godmother.*

# CONTENTS

# The Fairy Isle of Coosanure

ONCE UPON A TIME there was a very lovely island on a big lake right in the heart of Ireland. It was called Coosanure and it was splendid indeed. It was there that the Árd-Rí, or High King of all the fairy kingdoms in Ireland, held court. In the middle of the island was the beautiful castle in which the Royal family lived. Elves from all over Ireland had come, and with love and care built this castle. It looked like the end of a rainbow because of the coloured stones they used in their work. I am sure you have heard of 'the crock of gold at the end of a rainbow' and wondered if it were true. Well, in this case it was very true because of the gold in the castle treasury. Whenever a rainbow appeared, one end always rested on the castle and, because of the gold there, the saying 'gold at the end of a rainbow' became a popular belief among the fairy folk. The gardens, parks and lawns were tidily laid out and extended down to the waters of the lake. All around the castle grounds were the houses and lands of the subjects of the Árd-Rí. The houses were enchanting to look at, the gardens always full of sweet-scented flowers, the folk always nicely dressed, and the air was filled with music, singing and laughter. Truly it was a real fairyland.

Because the Árd-Rí lived here visitors to the island were ever coming and going. Fairy Kings from all over the land came to visit him. They came to ask his advice, to pay their respects or to bring him gifts, but always they came to see the wonder of his palace. Visits often lasted for days and in the evenings, when all the work was done, everyone joined in merrymaking, for fairy folk love to sing and dance and play sweet music. Carnivals such as Bealtaine and Samhain were held but the really important day was *Lá an Árd-Rí* or The High King's Day.

On this day a great Assembly was held. All the Kings of Ireland attended and each one had the right to speak. New laws were made, old laws were often changed. The Árd-Rí was a very wise ruler. He moved through the land visiting his people so he knew the way they lived and their special needs, which often changed with the years. He made sure that the laws were for the benefit of all and, in this way, when the Assembly came to an end everyone was happy. Although the Assembly lasted for only one day — from sunrise to sunset — there were three days set aside for preparations. These were called 'gathering days'. One can well imagine how delighted the visitors were to meet again, not having seen one another, maybe, since the last great feast.

Each visiting King brought a special gift to the Árd-Rí and it was the custom that these gifts be made of pure gold. The gifts always pleased the Árd-Rí, not so much because of their value, but because of the goodwill that came with them. All knew, of course, that the Árd-Rí was always generous to those in need and he used his gold freely to help others.

When the great Assembly ended the carnival really started. For three days the palace grounds were crowded. There was something for everyone — music, dancing, singing, games, great tables of food and drink (fruit drinks I may add, because fairies do not drink beer as mortals do). At night, because of the cool air, many open fires were lit.

It was a sight to behold — the magnificent castle, the shining moon at night, the elegantly dressed visitors, all combined with the music, laughter and song to make a true fairyland.

Everyone enjoyed themselves and all were sorry when the first of the 'scattering days' came. The first to come on 'gathering days' were the first to leave. All left in the order in which they had come. Farewells were made as one by one they left with the wish and the hope that the following year they would all meet again at another great Assembly. As each King left, the Árd-Rí gave him a gift and an invitation to return the following year.

The years passed, many, many of them and then one day after a great Assembly something happened. When the last of the visitors had gone a terrible discovery was made which was to bring great sorrow to the little Island. Little did anyone present know that they had been present at the last great Assembly on the Fairy Isle of Coosanure.

*The Árd-Rí's Celebration.*

*The Blue Diamond.*

# The Sorrow of Coosanure

AWAY BACK IN TIME a royal visitor from a far off land presented a superb Blue Diamond to the Fairy King of the Western Islands. It was a most treasured gift and of immense value, even in Fairyland where goodness is treasured above all. Treasures, gold and jewels are only secondary to love and goodwill there. Even so, the Blue Diamond was a precious gift — a bond between two Kingdoms, one in Ireland and the other in far away Spain. It was always kept in the Islands and many visitors came to see it.

One year, at a great Assembly, the King of the Western Islands was elected Árd-Rí of all the fairies of Ireland. It was a great honour for him, and both he and his subjects were very proud. Sadly, they realized that they would have to leave their three lovely islands off the West Coast and make their new life on the Isle of Coosanure. Being sea-loving fairies, life would be very different for them but they were prepared to sacrifice all to be with their King — the newly elected Árd-Rí.

When they finally moved to Coosanure the new Árd-Rí brought the Blue Diamond with him. He made a special law that the Blue Diamond was to be the symbol of the authority of the Árd-Rí, who would be its guardian. It was never to be taken from the Island and should anything happen to it, be it stolen, lost or sold, a great misfortune would befall the island and its people. A special casket was made and inside it was put a special message to be read by the reigning Árd-Rí only if something were to happen to the Blue Diamond.

Down along the years this casket had a place of honour in the palace throne-room. A fine glass case was made for the Diamond and it was never taken out of this casket except on the great Assembly day. Then, it was worn by the reigning Árd-Rí. When the ceremonies were over, it was put back in the case for another

11

*The King with the Scroll of Doom.*

At sunset on the day following the loss of the Blue Diamond the Isle of Coosanure will sink into the waters of the lake and will remain there forever unless the spell is broken by the return of the Blue Diamond. Once every year the island will rise to the surface of the lake. If on that day between

year. Many Árd-Rís had come and gone and then one day, the day after a great Assembly, it was discovered that the Blue Diamond was missing. Without it the Árd-Rí had no authority to rule. The palace was in an uproar. Where had it gone? Who had taken it? Was it one of the visitors? All these questions and many more were asked, but no one could answer them.

The Blue Diamond had to be found before sunset because, if not, a great misfortune would fall upon the Árd-Rí, the people and the Island. The search began, everyone took part. Every nook and cranny was explored but no diamond was to be found. The visitors had all gone and it was too late to contact them again before sunset, for, even in Fairyland, magic is not strong enough to reach out to everyone.

The day passed slowly. The search continued and at sunset everyone knew that since the diamond had not been found the spell would take effect next day. One by one, everyone retired for the night. The moon never shone more brightly, the flowers never smelled more lovely and the castle looked like a jewel resting on a green cushion, but it was an island of sadness — no music, no dancing, no laughter. For the first time Coosanure, the beautiful Coosanure, was quiet and lonely.

13

Next morning at sunrise the Árd-Rí called all his subjects together on the lawn in front of the Royal Palace. He told them that since the Blue Diamond had not been found, he must now open the casket and see what was in store for them. The casket was brought forward and opened. The Árd-Rí took out the paper and read it. All could see how troubled he looked and it was to a silent audience that he raised his hand asking for everyone to listen carefully to what he had to say. Before he could do so, one of the fairies asked that he be allowed to speak. When his wish was granted, he came forward, saluted his Árd-Rí and spoke so that all could hear. 'My message is all too short. I do not know of the contents of the paper, but I believe that a spell is about to be put on the Árd-Rí. Whatever happens to the Árd-Rí should be shared by us. Whatever happens to him, happens to us. Wherever he goes, we go. His lot is our lot.'

Turning again to the crowd on the lawn he said, 'Do you agree?' With a shout that could be heard a long, long way off the people cried again and again, 'Whatever happens to you, happens to us. Wherever you go — we go. Your lot is our lot. We are agreed on that.'

The Árd-Rí was deeply moved by their loyalty and thanked them for it. Then he started to read.

'At sunset on the day following the loss of the Blue Diamond the Isle of Coosanure will sink into the waters of the lake and will remain there forever unless the spell is broken by the return of the Blue Diamond. Once every year the island will rise to the surface of the lake. If on that day between sunrise and sunset the Blue Diamond is returned to its rightful place, the spell will be broken and life on the island will return to normal. If the Diamond is not returned and the spell not broken, then at sunset the island will sink once more into the lake for another year.'

There was a hushed silence as the meaning of this awful spell became clear. The Árd-Rí continued, 'The fault is mine. I could not let you all share this punishment. I want you all — every one of you — to leave the island today. I will stay on alone. It is the least I can do for you who have been so loyal to me and to mine throughout the years.'

*The sinking Island.*

The crowds, who had been so silent, now rose as one body and said, 'No, we will not leave. We will stay and share your sorrow. Loyalty goes two ways — our loyalty is no greater than yours. We will stay.'

That evening at sunset the spell took effect. Slowly, very slowly the Isle of Coosanure began to sink into the clear waters of the lake. Down, down it went until even the highest towers of the castle could no longer be seen.

Life under water went on as before except that there were no visits from other Kings and their Courts, nor was there a *Lá an Árd-Rí,* and this everyone missed very much. Still, they were happy enough as they had their own feasts and enjoyed music and song. Even at the height of their feasts it was noticed that their music had a slow sweet sound — the music of love and sorrow and acceptance, all of which gave peace to those who played it and those who heard it.

To those who did not know of the spell, Coosanure was no more. But it is said that on clear nights, when the moon shines high, the castle could be seen shining through the bright waters and haunting fairy music could even be heard. Many years passed and each year for one day the island appeared at sunrise only to sink at sunset. It was on one of these days that the next episode begins.

# Paudeen and Conn the Cobbler

ANOTHER YEAR PASSED, and another day of hope dawned for the fairy folk of Coosanure. As the sun rose over the lake the Fairy Isle rose majestically from the clear waters and lay shimmering in the morning light. As in other years all work had been done so that everyone could enjoy the holiday in the sun. There was always the hope that the island would remain above the waters. In the meantime they made merry, for no matter how long the day was, it was all too short for the folk of Coosanure. There was music, dancing, singing, sports, games and feasting. No one stayed indoors. The lawns and parks were thronged with fairies, elves, and leprechauns, all enjoying themselves to the full. The Royal Family were out too, mixing with the crowd, and it was noticed that the Árd-Rí, once so happy among his subjects, was now silent and sad. No one blamed him for what had happened and although he was content with his lot under the water, his distress affected him terribly each year when the Island rose above the water.

On this day, the young Prince was with the Árd-Rí and his Queen and was having a great time. Because he was so young and so good humoured he was a favourite among the people. He played around with the other boys of his own age and in the excitement strayed away from his parents. He visited this house and that, spoke to the old folk, skipped with the fairy girls, who were all in love with him, and generally had a great time. Then, suddenly, he felt tired and looked around for a place to rest. He was quite near a little pond, and knowing that there were seats there, he went towards it. Beside the pond he saw several white cushions and ran towards them. First he climbed onto a wall, then he stepped on to one of the cushions and there, although he tried hard to keep his eyes open, he soon fell fast asleep. The excitement had been too much for him so he slept soundly as the sun sank lower and lower

17

*'The Little One' asleep on a swan's back.*

in the sky. Soon it was down to the rim of the lake and then it vanished altogether. The Blue Diamond had not been found, so the spell had not been broken and the Island too sank slowly into the waters for another year.

All this time the little Prince lay fast asleep on what he thought was a white cushion. Of course it was not a white cushion but one of four swans who had stopped to rest on their journey to another lake in Ireland. As the Island began to sink the swans took to the air and, after flying for some time, came to a lake where they were to spend many years. The Prince was so small and light that the swan never knew of the little load nesting on her back between the feathers. When the swans came to rest on the shore of the lake the Prince awoke. He looked around for a while and then slid to the ground. He had been asleep for a long time and, like all little boys, was hungry. He started to run back to the Palace but very soon found that everything was strange to him. There were no parks and no lawns; there was no castle, and above all there were no people. Everything was so quiet. Being very young, it was a while before he realized that he was lost and that he did not know where to go. Other boys might get frightened but not so 'the little one', for was he not a Prince and a brave one too?

As he was hungry he looked around for something to eat. He knew that if he found a house he would get food, and that the kindly people in the house would bring him back to the castle — but he could not find a house. He knew that he could eat certain berries, but it was too early for wild strawberries or blackberries so his search was in vain. The sun was high in the sky when he came to a small road. He felt happier, because wherever there is a road there is bound to be a house. He forgot his hunger and his feeling of being lost and skipped along the road. Very soon he saw a quaint cottage in the distance. He reached the gate and was about to enter when he heard someone coming up the road from the far side. It was an old man coming towards him, bent with the weight of his two bags which seemed to be very heavy. Overjoyed at seeing someone at last, and being a kindly boy, his first thought was to help carry one of the heavy bags. He ran towards the old man. To his great surprise the old man, who looked up and saw this strange figure running towards him, started to shout, 'Go away! Go away!' The Prince stopped short on the road. He was terrified. No one had ever spoken like this to him. He was tired

19

hungry, lost and now this! It was too much for him and for the first time in his life he started to cry.

The little old man was also terrified. He thought that this stranger was about to rob him of his food and drink, but now the little stranger was crying. This was very strange indeed. Being a kindly man he left down the bags and approached the boy and said, 'There now, little one, don't cry, everything will be alright. You surprised me and as I did not know who you were, or what you were going to do, I too was frightened. Come along to my cottage and we can talk!' The little Prince stopped crying, smiled at the old man and took up one of the bags. As they went up the garden path he remembered seeing little old men working in his father's castle and they were very like this old man. The Prince did not know then that a new life was about to start for him and that this old man was going to be his best friend.

When they were inside the cottage, the old man asked many questions, most of which the Prince could not answer. After a short while the old man put on some milk and made a meal of milk, honey and bread. The little Prince ate everything put before him; then, putting his head down on the table, he was soon fast asleep.

While he was sleeping the old man made up a tiny bed and lifted him on to it, covering him with a rug. He sat beside the bed for a long time, staring at this little one who had come so strangely into his life. He kept remembering that long years before he had helped an old lady. In gratitude she said, 'When you are old, a little wee stranger will come into your life in a curious way and you will become great friends. Your days will always be happy with him.' Maybe this boy was the stranger. Tomorrow they would talk. He would be rested then and able to answer all the questions that he wanted to ask. Tomorrow would be early enough.

Next morning the Prince woke early. He looked around the strange room. He got up and began to explore the cottage. In another room he found the old man sleeping on a small bed. He trod softly for fear of waking him. He opened another door and entered a big room. There on a bench he saw lots and lots of shoes. All around the room were shelves laden with shoes and boxes of buckles and coloured buttons. He saw rolls of coloured leather, colours of all kinds. He remembered a similar room at the castle and remembered too that old men, just like his new friend,

20

*Paudeen meets Conn the Cobbler.*

*Looking around Conn's workshop.*

worked there as shoemakers. This, then, was a shoemaker's workshop. What he did not know was that this was the workshop of Conn the Cobbler, the most famous cobbler in all Fairyland. While looking around he heard a noise. It was the old man coming into the room. He smiled at the Prince and said, 'Go now and wash and dress, then we shall have a meal and afterwards a talk. You can tell me all you know and then we will know what to do. You may stay here for as long as you like. In the meantime, you may come and go as you please.'

After the meal Conn asked the Prince many questions. The Prince told him all he knew which was not very much and was very confusing. He was too young to know of the spell on the Fairy Isle, and why it disappeared beneath the waters of the lake. He did not know he was a Prince. He only knew that he was in a strange place and that the cobbler was a very nice friend to have. So, for the time being he was happy enough.

The two got on well together and later when the old man said, 'I'm Conn the Cobbler', the Prince said, 'I'm the little one'. Conn said, 'You'll have to have a real name so I'm going to call you – Paudeen'. Until he found out more about him, Conn thought it better to say nothing to anyone about this boy who called himself 'the little one'. He decided to keep it a secret and the Prince agreed with him, thinking it was part of a game.

That is how the two of them started off as friends – Conn the Cobbler and Paudeen, the fairy Prince. Paudeen, as we now call him, did not move away from the cottage. Conn went to the fairy village to get all the provisions. When Paudeen was a little older Conn would take him to the village to meet boys and girls of his own age.

Time passed quickly for Conn and Paudeen. They became great friends and while Conn made many many pairs of shoes, Paudeen learned to keep house. He could now light fires, prepare meals and keep all the rooms tidy. In his spare time, he worked in the garden and besides growing vegetables, he had a great love for flowers. In time, the air was filled with the scent of the colourful flowers he had grown. Sometimes the scent reminded him of somewhere but he could not remember where. Time had blotted out the memory of other days and, except for occasional reminders of another life, he grew up happy with Conn and his new life in the cottage. But there were others who remembered him and never forgot the little

*Fairies, elves and leprechauns making Paudeen's new clothes.*

one who vanished on one of the days when the Isle of Coosanure appeared on the lake at sunrise only to sink again at sunset because the spell was not broken.

Shall we go back and visit them for a short while? When we were last in the Isle of Coosanure the air was filled with laughter, music and song. Everyone was enjoying the sunshine and the festivities of the day all hoped that by some lucky chance the spell would be broken and their lives would return to normal with their Island resting on top of the waters rather than beneath. The Árd-Rí and his family were about to return to the castle when it was discovered that the 'little one' was not with them. At first no-one minded much for he was thought to be with friends and so would come to no harm. However, as time passed and he did not show up, a search was made and to everyone's horror he could not be found. The music stopped; the laughter died down; even the sun did not seem to shine so brightly. They all started searching now. The sun was going down slowly and time was running out. Where could he be? His little friends were asked but could not tell much. 'He was playing with us and then he left us. We thought he had gone back to the castle.' No one had seen him go towards the little pond and no one knew that he had rested on the swan's back. Soon, too soon, the sun was down on the rim of the lake but the search continued, the searchers hoping against hope that the little Prince would be found. But it was not to be and as the Island began to sink beneath the waters of the lake a cry went up from all the people. It was the first time that such sadness was witnessed in Fairyland and they could do little else but mourn the loss of the little one who was beloved by all. They did not know that this trick of fate would mean that some day their sorrow would be turned to joy. They could not see that then and, as the last tower of the castle sank beneath the waters, their cries of sorrow were so great that people far away heard what was known for a long time afterwards as the 'crying wind'.

Life went on in the cottage. Time passed quickly and Conn saw that Paudeen was growing very big. He decided to share his secret with others and to ask for their help. One day he went to the village and spent most of the day there, Paudeen looking after the house and garden. Funnily enough while Paudeen loved looking at Conn making such beautiful shoes, he could never enjoy making them as Conn had hoped he would. Conn had a great secret, a secret known to very few. Besides being the best cobbler in Fairyland, he was the only one who could make magic shoes. He had hoped to pass on the secret to Paudeen but Paudeen had no love for cobbling, so Conn kept the secret to himself.

When Conn came back from the village it was nearly bed time. Paudeen had supper ready, the house clean and tidy. They sat down and had a meal and then retired to bed. Paudeen knew that Conn had good news of some sort but said nothing, knowing that Conn would tell it in his own good time. Soon Paudeen who had worked hard in his garden was sound asleep. Next morning he woke rather late, and feeling guilty he jumped out of bed and reached for his clothes. Imagine his surprise when instead of finding his own clothes there, he found white trousers and jacket, a shirt and stockings, and a leather belt with a golden buckle. He was at a loss to know where they came from until he remembered that Conn was very pleased with himself the night before. It was Conn who had bought the clothes in the village. He quickly washed himself and put on the new clothes. They fitted perfectly and when he saw himself in the mirror he was delighted.

He ran out of the room and into the big kitchen to thank Conn but got a great surprise to find that the place was crowded with fairies, elves and leprechauns from the village. He was so surprised that he stopped just inside the door. Conn was in the middle of the crowd and looked pleased. Then all began to laugh and shouted together, 'Welcome Paudeen, we are very happy to have you as our friend.' Paudeen did not know whether to laugh or cry. He felt great in his new clothes and now he had new friends. He moved into the room and began thanking each one for their offer of friendship and then, turning to Conn, he thanked him for the beautiful clothes. Conn had to stop him. 'Paudeen,' he said, 'I did not give you the new clothes. I went into the village yesterday and told them about you. Everyone wanted to help so they made up a plan. They came here last night and spent all their time in spinning the yarns and making the cloth and then the suit. You are not one of us but you are welcome all the same. That is the reason why your suit is made of white. Wherever you go you will be made welcome for you have been good to me and my friends know it. A friend of mine is a friend of theirs. Tomorrow I will make you a splendid pair of shoes. Then someday we will visit the Palace and there you will meet the King. Now we will have a meal.'

It was only then that Paudeen saw the table laid out for a party. It was a welcome party for him and they all sat down together happy in the thought that they had done a good turn and made a new friend. Paudeen was never so happy before and, as he put his arms around Conn and thanked him for everything, Conn knew that the little stranger was the one he had been told about many years before. This was to be his friend in old age. It was a great reward for the kindness that he had shown to an old lady in need many years before.

Everyone present took the day off, returning to the village where Paudeen met all the villagers and got a very special welcome. That night before he went to sleep he went over the day in his mind and vowed that he would always help his good friend Conn and the fairy folk in the village.

# Paudeen meets Finula

IT WAS A GAY SUMMER EVENING and the sun, sinking in a big red ball, sent sunbeams all over the land. Having worked hard during the day, Paudeen decided to visit his friends in the village. He had washed, dressed in his new suit, and was wearing the new shoes that Conn had made for him. Both of them were proud of the new shoes, made of white leather with two specially designed buckles. No one else had shoes like them. Why? I'll let you in on the secret — they were magic shoes, that's why! Yes, real magic shoes!! Conn had made them, told Paudeen the secret and told him how to use their magical power when he was in need. One thing was very important. The magic could only be used for good, either for himself or for someone else in need. If they were asked to do bad or evil things the magic would not work and the shoes would get smaller and smaller so that no-one could wear them again. Paudeen promised Conn that he would use the magic only in great need and only for good.

As he skipped along the path that led to the village he stopped suddenly, thinking that he had heard a voice. Then he heard it again but it was not so much a voice as a sob. He looked around and could not see anyone. After a while he heard the voice again and this time he could hear it quite plainly. It said: 'Oh what am I going to do? Will someone please help me?'

After a search he found a little fairy girl sitting on a rose bush crying as if her heart were breaking. Paudeen asked her what was wrong, and if he could help. The girl looked up at the strange boy dressed in white and because Paudeen looked kindly at her, she said in a very quiet voice: 'I am Finula, Princess of the Sunbeam Fairies. I was flying around and saw a lovely dewdrop on a rose. It was quite warm and I decided to have a bath. I took off my wings and bathed myself in the dewdrop. When I finished I could not find my wings. I've searched everywhere and I cannot find them.

29

*Paudeen wearing his magic shoes.*

The sun is going down soon and if I cannot get my wings I cannot fly up to the sunbeam which would take me to my father's castle on the hill. If the sun goes down before I get home I can never return to my home again for everyone must be home by sunset.'

Paudeen felt sorry for her. 'I will help you if I can, but first let us search for them.' They did so but it was no use, the wings could not be found. Paudeen wanted to help but didn't know what to do. Suddenly, he remembered the magic shoes. Turning to Finula he said, 'I'll be back shortly but trust in me. If I can help I'll do so, but do not move from where you are.' With that he moved out of her sight and, bending down, he turned each buckle around three turns to the left and three times to the right, saying at the same time, 'Someone is in need, please help me to help her'. No sooner had he the words said than he was lifted off his feet. Away down the path he sped, over trees, hills and rivers, until he came to a big mound beside a clump of trees. He was lowered gently and saw that the ground nearby was covered with gossamer web. It was a spider colony. Spiders are grand little things, you know. Some people don't like them, others hate them, but people shouldn't form opinions like that about spiders because they never harm anyone — except maybe flies and insects and we could do without the flies which often carry disease. Spiders spin their webs, live their own lives and don't bother much with what goes on in the big outside world.

Anyway, a big spider, bigger than all the other spiders on the mound, came over to Paudeen and said, 'We were expecting you. Fairy wings are very hard to get so we have spun a pair of gossamer ones for your friend. Take them back very quickly or it will be too late.' Paudeen took the wings and before he started back he said to the spider, whose name was Spinner, 'Someday I will repay your kindness. I don't know how or when but I promise you I will not forget your good deed'. Spinner said, 'Yes, someday we will need your help and we know that you will not fail us — but hurry or your friend will be beyond help.'

Paudeen thanked him again and waved good-bye to the other spiders. Again he was lifted off his feet and sped over the rivers, trees and hills to the little path beside the rose tree. Finula was waiting anxiously and was overjoyed to see him. They quickly fastened on the wings and soon she was flying around and around. Before she flew up to the last sunbeam she said to Paudeen, 'What

*Paudeen meets Finula.*

*Spinner gives Paudeen a pair of gossamer wings for Finula.*

is your name and where do you live?' Paudeen told her, 'My name is Paudeen and I live with Conn the Cobbler, but hurry on or you will not get up to your sunbeam — see, it is fading fast.' Finula said, 'Thanks again — remember I will not forget your kind deed.' With that she flew up to the sunbeam and was soon on her way to the castle on the hill.

Paudeen felt so happy that he was able to do a good deed and after his visit to the village, told Conn about the whole affair. Conn was pleased that Paudeen was able to do good and was sure that he would only use the magic shoes to help out someone in need of help.

Indeed, we will learn later that Finula — Princess Finula — did not forget Paudeen and his good deed.

# The King's Gift

CONN THE COBBLER had been very busy in his workshop for many weeks past. Now, he had no more leather or fancy buckles, and he still had many, many shoes to make. You see, it was coming up to Bealtaine, one of the great fairy festivals, and everyone in the village wanted new shoes. As he looked at row after row of lovely coloured shoes he could not help thinking of how generous Paudeen was in helping him out. Paudeen had no great love for leatherwork, but to help Conn he spent all his time during the past month in the workshop. From sunrise to sunset they worked away only taking time to have their meals which were prepared by Oisin — a nephew of Conn — who came for a short stay but loved it so much that he stayed on and on.

Let me tell you about Oisin. He was small and fat and forever in good humour. Every morning after breakfast he would say, 'Another day Uncle Conn?', and Conn would say, 'Well, we will see how today goes!' In that way Oisin stayed on and on and really loved the place. As Conn and Paudeen worked in the workshop, Oisin kept house. He prepared the meals, made the beds, kept the fire going and tended to the garden. He had one little fault — that is if you could call it a fault. He was careless and gay, a real happy-go-lucky leprechaun. Life to him was such fun. He was very good at whatever work he had to do. But when the work was done and he sat down day-dreaming, well, one could not know what to expect. Such day-dreaming got him into the bad books with Conn, but not for long. Conn always forgave. Oisin's greatest fault was that, often, he never stopped to think and it was on one such occasion that he caused quite an upset for his good friends, Uncle Conn and Paudeen — you will see what I mean as we go on with our story.

It came as no surprise when Conn announced at supper time that on the next day, after breakfast, he would have to go to a village a good distance away for more leather and further on to get the fancy buckles. Paudeen, being the good boy he was, would not let Conn go on his own. He told Conn, 'You go to the village for the leather. I will go on further for the buckles.' In that way they could get both leather and buckles the same day and be back before sunset! Conn was delighted with the plan and at breakfast the next morning he told Oisin, 'I am going away for the day but if anyone calls for me say I'll be back at sunset. You can take the day off from your usual work, but be sure to have a fire and a hot meal for us when we come back at sunset.' Oisin was delighted that Conn had placed so much trust in him and as the others left, he promised that all would be well when they returned.

He set to work straight away and gave the cottage a real spring cleaning. After his mid-day meal he set a fire for the evening and then, locking the cottage, he went into the village to play with his friends there. In the evening he had a meal with them and then went back to the cottage. He was going to surprise Conn and Paudeen by cooking something special for them. He was about to light the fire when he heard voices outside. Always a little bit inquisitive, he went to the door and saw two well-dressed strangers standing outside the garden gate. They were talking in low tones and when they saw Oisin they called out to him, 'We are looking for the cottage of Conn the Cobbler!' Oisin ran down the garden path, saying at the same time, 'This is Conn the Cobbler's cottage.' The two men looked pleased and then one of them said, 'Do you live here?'

Oisin said 'Yes, I do. Conn is away and will not be back until sunset.' Then he noticed a small beautiful red car behind the two men. He was fascinated by it and asked, 'Can I see the lovely car?'

'Of course you can,' one of the men said. 'This car is for you.'

'For me?' said Oisin.

'Yes,' said the man. 'The King of Tír na Gréine sent it to you with his best wishes and grateful thanks.' He went on, 'You will have no trouble with it. It goes on air — needs no lights, because it shines in the dark — no horn, because when it moves bells ring automatically. We hope you will have a very nice time driving yourself and Conn around the country. It's a pity we cannot see Conn, the most famous cobbler in Fairyland who makes such wonderful shoes.' They said their goodbyes to Oisin who barely spoke to them, he was so excited about the car.

*Oisin with the King's gift — a car that goes on air and needs no lights.*

Poor little Oisin — careless and gay as usual, he never stopped to think. He might have asked himself, 'Why did the King send me a car? — and with his best wishes and thanks? I do not know of the King of Tír na Gréine.' Alas! poor Oisin did not stop to think. He was so excited that in a flash he was in the car and off he went, car shining, bells ringing. He forgot about the fire and the supper — indeed he forgot to lock the door of the cottage.

He was gone a short while when the strange men came back again. One of them called out several times but, oddly enough, he was calling, 'Paudeen, Paudeen.' Getting no reply, he entered the cottage and left an envelope on the table saying, 'When he comes back he will find it,' and off they went down the road again.

Well, the sun was sinking low in the skies when Conn and Paudeen arrived back at the cottage. Conn was surprised when Oisin did not come out to meet them. He was amazed when he found that the door of the cottage was open and that there was no fire — no meal — but above all no Oisin. Both of them were tired and hungry and were at a loss to know what was wrong. Then Conn saw the envelope on the table. 'This will explain everything,' he said, but when he took up the envelope he said in a hushed voice, 'Paudeen, this letter is for you. It's from the Royal Palace of Tír na Gréine!' Paudeen took the envelope, broke the seal and took out the card. 'Conn,' he said, 'This is an invitation from the King. It is an invitation for you and I to attend the Grand Ball tonight. It is the King's wish that we go, so let us wash and change and get ready. We can have something to eat when we get there. We can leave a message for Oisin — wherever he is — and tell him we will be back at sunrise.'

Conn was delighted for Paudeen's sake about the invitation but he was old and tired. 'You go, Paudeen. Thank the King for me. He will understand. Old people understand one another. I am too tired just now but tell the King that I respect his wishes and will go and see him soon. I'll make supper for myself and Oisin. When he comes back he will tell me what happened. I'll tell him where you have gone. Hurry now, off you go and enjoy yourself.'

Paudeen understood. Conn was tired but that was not all. Conn wanted to be at home when Oisin came back. Before he left for the Palace however, he lit the fire, prepared a meal for Conn, and tucked him into his warm bed. He was not worried very much about Oisin. Some little misunderstanding had cropped up and he felt sure he would be home soon.

Going out of the cottage he bent low and rubbed his magic shoes in the way that Conn had told him, saying as he did, 'Take me to the Palace of Tír na Gréine.' Soon he was skimming over hill and dale and away up to the gates of the Palace. Although it was night time when he left the cottage, the sun was shining at the palace. It is always shining there — that is why it is called Tír na Gréine, the land of the sun.

At the Palace gates he handed up his invitation. Soon he was inside and was taken to a small room for a light meal. The banquet, he was told, would begin later on but in the meantime he was free to enjoy himself in the Palace grounds. After the meal Paudeen made his way to the gardens where everyone was relaxing. It was his first time in Tír na Gréine and he was enchanted by it all. Fairy music filled the air and dancing, singing and laughing fairies, elves and leprechauns crowded the lawns. Everyone took part in the entertainment — everyone was happy.

He had expected to be taken to the King, but no one treated him as a stranger. Indeed he was accepted as a friend and one little fairy girl caught him by the hand and invited him to join her circle of boys and girls. Delighted, he danced and sang and laughed with them and enjoyed it to the full. After quite a time with them, he saw a Palace guard standing at the door of the castle. Excusing himself to his new friends, he left the circle and spoke to the guard, introducing himself and asking to be brought to the King. The royal guard said, 'I'm so glad I have found you. His Majesty has been asking for you for some time. Please come with me.'

They entered the Palace and walked down a long corridor lined with court officials to the door of the Throne Room. As Paudeen waited at the door to be introduced, he had a chance to look around. The room was crowded but there was a passage between the people down the centre. He could see a throne on which the King was seated. Beside him was the Queen on another throne and on both sides of them were the Prince and his sister, Princess Finula. Guests from the other Royal Houses sat on both sides of the now crowded room. Paudeen had never seen anything like it.

As he walked down the passage to the throne, all present started to clap their hands and made him welcome. He stopped before the throne and bowed to the King and then to the Queen — and was surprised when the King spoke rather crossly. 'Why was Paudeen

*Two bodyguards arrest Paudeen.*

not brought before us when he arrived? He is our special guest of honour. I wish to thank him for his kindly act to our Princess Finula. He should have been brought here as soon as he arrived. I am very annoyed.'

Paudeen, afraid that he would get someone into trouble, said, 'Your Majesty, if anyone is at fault it was me. When I entered the palace grounds and I saw all the gaiety, the dancing, singing, and music, I'm afraid I joined in the merrymaking. I felt that I had seen something like this before, but I cannot say where, or when. I enjoyed myself and had a real happy time. I'm afraid that it was I that was at fault.'

The King smiled at him so Paudeen continued. He thanked the King for his invitation, and then made apologies for Conn, giving the reason why he did not come. The King said, 'I understand. Conn is getting old like myself. Later on I will arrange that we meet.'

Paudeen then bowed and backed away. The King looked at him with a quizzical smile. Paudeen wondered what he was to do now. A silence fell on the room and everyone seemed to be uncomfortable. After what seemed to be a long time the King turned his back on Paudeen and called to one of his guards. 'Take this boy away. Take him to the punishment room – no, take him to the guest room and I will see later as to what I am to do.'

Two of the bodyguards took Paudeen by the arms and led him away through the door he had first entered, along a passage and into a big room. There were tables and chairs and a fire in the hearth. Bookshelves lined the wall and it was very comfortable indeed. One of the bodyguards spoke to Paudeen. 'I am sorry I have to lock the door. You are not permitted to talk to anyone except the Royal family. You will have a meal brought to you but you are not to speak to anyone other than their Highnesses if they come to see you.'

Before they left they took away his shoes and cap and then he was all alone. In the distance he could hear the music and laughter. It all seemed so far away for poor lonely Paudeen. Here he was locked up in this room and he did not know for what reason. He went over everything in his mind but it was no use. Had he offended the King? No, he had paid his respects. Still the King seemed to be angry. Why was he angry? Why was he being punished like this? Oh, if only Conn was here to advise him, he would know what to do, but Conn was far away and Paudeen felt all alone.

A meal was brought but he was in no humour for eating and left the meal untouched. He felt very tired and before long he dozed off to sleep in the big armchair beside the fire. How long he slept he did not know but he was awakened by someone calling his name. When he opened his eyes he saw his little friend, Princess Finula, sitting opposite him. Paudeen brightened up when he saw her. He knew that she was there to help him and would explain why he was here.

'I am so glad to see you, Paudeen, but am sorry for what has happened. The King was very cross with you. You will have to stay here for quite a long time — maybe until Samhain. Then you will be taken before the court of the Kings and maybe banished from Fairyland. Oh, Paudeen! What will you do then? I'm so sorry for you and I am powerless to help you. It's the law of the Kingdom and I cannot interfere. You will be well looked after while you are here. I will come and visit you whenever I can and will bring my friends too.'

Paudeen was getting more and more surprised, more and more shocked. He kept silent all the while that Finula was talking. Then he got up and spoke gently to her. 'Finula,' he said, 'I am truly sorry for all that has happened. I cannot understand what I have done wrong. I never meant to displease the King. I would not give offence to anyone and surely not to my host, no matter who that host might be. You must know that, Finula. Please tell me how I have offended the King. Please help me for I am so miserable.'

Finula looked at him for a short while. She was really sorry for the little friend who helped her when she was so frightened so far away from home. Gently she said, 'Paudeen, you seemed un-gracious to the King. He was very proud of you for helping me. The little magic car he sent you was a very special gift. No one in this kingdom has one like it. Everyone in Tír na Gréine knew of this car which the King had made specially for you and all were waiting for you to thank him for this lovely gift. When you did not do so, the King was very upset. He had spoken so highly of you to all the court and then he felt as if he had been wrong about you. You did not mention his gift — did not even thank him. To act like that to him in the presence of all the court was a great offence. Oh Paudeen! What came over you? Why did you not thank him publicly? He would have been so proud to hear you tell of the

43

wonderful car.'

Paudeen kept his eyes on Finula all the time she was speaking, shaking his head from side to side. 'Finula,' he whispered, 'oh, Finula, Finula, what car do you speak of? I know of no car. Please tell me, Finula. I do not know what you speak of. I am so unhappy. Please tell me what is wrong?'

Again Finula looked at him without speaking. She rose and walked around the room in deep thought. Then she told Paudeen all she knew — all that she had been told. The King had a special car made for Paudeen as a gift for helping her at the rose tree. It was delivered by two of the King's messengers as well as the invitation to the Grand Ball.

'If you got one, you must have got the other as both had been delivered to Conn's cottage. They were there at Conn's cottage early yesterday.'

Paudeen could hardly believe his ears. Now he stood up and gazed into the fire. Then it all came to him in a flash. He knew now why Oisin was not at the cottage when Conn and himself arrived home. He believed that Oisin was driving around in the car. That was why the cottage door was left open and why there was no fire, no hot meal. Oisin had got so excited when he saw the car that he went off for a drive forgetting everything else.

Paudeen begged Finula to sit with him. Together at the fire he told her what he thought had happened. He had been away all day with Conn. He told her about the invitation left on the table. That was the reason why he came to the Ball. He did not know about the car. He did not see any car. He came to the Ball because the King had invited him and because he wished to see her once more. But he said, ' There must be some mistake. Oisin would never take anything that did not belong to him. Oisin is careless and gay but good at heart. If he did go away in the car there must be a good reason. The King's messengers did deliver the invitation, but, what about the car? Did they really deliver the car to the cottage, to the right cottage? If they did not, then where is Oisin — why did he leave the cottage?'

Finula heard all this with growing excitement. 'Say no more, Paudeen — we'll soon get to the bottom of this mystery. Oh I'm so glad! I knew that you were not what you seemed to be. Be patient — I'll be back soon.'

She came back with the King's two messengers who had been at

*The King forgives Paudeen and Oisin.*

45

Conn's cottage the day before. 'Look well,' said Finula, 'Did you ever see this leprechaun before?' One of them said, 'Yes, Princess, I saw him dancing on the lawn last night before the Ball.'

'But did you ever see him before?'

'No, I cannot say I have.'

Finula turned to the other messenger. 'And you, did you ever see him before?'

'No, Your Highness, I never saw him before. He is a stranger to me!'

'That is very strange indeed,' said Finula, 'for this is the one to whom you were to deliver the car and the invitation at Conn's cottage. You told the King that you delivered both to the cottage saying how excited the leprechaun was and how happy he was to receive it.'

The messengers looked at one another and then tried to speak together. 'Your Highness, we did deliver the car and the invitation as we were ordered — but this is not the one that was at the cottage. The leprechaun at the cottage was small and fat, a real happy little leprechaun. He said he lived with Conn the Cobbler. It was to him we delivered the car. When we left we had forgotten the invitation. We went back to deliver it and he was gone in the car — so we left the invitation on the table.'

'What nonsense is this I hear?' said a voice from the door. It was the King who had heard all that was said and was now more annoyed than ever. 'Go at once,' he roared. 'At once I say. Go to the cottage — bring back the little car and the one that received it. No more talk now. A great wrong has been done to Paudeen and I mean to make it up to him. Come with me Paudeen, and you too Finula.'

They all left for the throne room and the King ordered that all the court assemble at mid-day.

Just before noon the messengers arrived back and with them was a very frightened Oisin. When he saw Paudeen, he felt relieved. He knew that whatever was wrong — and at this time he did not know — Paudeen would stand by him.

The whole court was now assembled and the messengers, Paudeen and Oisin stood in front of the King. 'First I'll hear the messengers and then I'll hear from you, Oisin,' he said, in a voice that frightened them all.

The messengers told their story and when they finished, the

46

King said to Oisin, 'Well, little one, what have you to say?'

Oisin looked at Paudeen and then at the King. 'Your Majesty,' he whispered, 'If I have done wrong I did not mean to. The messengers have told you the truth. When they asked me was this Conn the Cobbler's cottage, I said yes. They asked me did I live here and I said yes. Then this messenger' – pointing at the taller of the two – 'said this car is for you. It is a present from the King of Tír na Gréine who sends it with his good wishes and thanks. He never mentioned Paudeen. He must have thought that because I lived with Conn that I was Paudeen. Because I was so excited about the lovely car, I never thought of saying why should the King send me a beautiful car as a gift and with his best thanks? The car was so nice – well, I got excited and when your messengers moved away I got into the car and went for a spin. It was really great and I forgot everything else and drove around and around. I even forgot about Conn and Paudeen. I forgot to lock the cottage door and forgot to have a hot meal for them when they came back. I am truly sorry for all the trouble I have caused your Majesty and Paudeen who is my best friend. Punish me if you must but please do not punish Paudeen. I know that he would be the last to give offence to anyone. If the messengers made a mistake I was the cause. If I had not gone off I would have seen that the invitation was addressed to Paudeen. I would have known then that they were looking for Paudeen and not for me. Please do not punish them. Everything was my fault.' He looked up at the King, tears in his eyes and whispered, 'I'm sorry, so sorry. Please forgive me.'

The King was deeply moved by the little fat leprechaun who stood before him. He called Oisin to him and put his arm around him. Addressing the court, he said: 'Oisin, I was going to deal severely with you. Because of your foolishness, you caused a great upset to me and to our friend Paudeen. I am going to forgive you – not because I am getting soft-hearted. No, I forgive you because you have told the truth, taking the blame for everything, but above all because you pleaded for Paudeen and the messengers. All is forgiven and to make up for the trouble I've caused to Paudeen I am going to have another Grand Ball. Paudeen will be the guest of honour and I want you to come and to bring my good friend Conn as well.'

So ended another chapter in the life of our little friend Paudeen.

He was to have many exciting times in the future as we shall see in further stories about this little leprechaun so loved by all.

# The Parting

LIFE IN THE FAIRY KINGDOM had been very happy for our
friends. Oisin had come to stay for good and Conn, now very
old, was glad to have his help in the running of the cottage.
Paudeen was now a fine young man and was a great favourite with
everyone. He was always considerate to others, kind to the old
folk, friendly to the little ones who loved him so much. He loved
sports, dancing, singing and happiness. All the girls were in love
with him, and although he was friendly to them all, no one could
say that he liked any one of them in particular. They all knew
that he had eyes only for Princess Finula from the kingdom of
Tír na Gréine and although she never spoke of it, everyone knew
that she loved Paudeen in return. He loved being in her company
whether in her own palace, where he was always welcome, or at
the fairy feasts in Clonfin.

They were a very happy couple and although everything seemed
to go well for them, there was a little something that prevented
their happiness from being complete, and the sad part was that
everyone except Paudeen knew the reason. You see, it was like
this — no, that would be unfair. I'll let it develop step by step as
the story goes so that you may understand it all the better.

Just at this time Paudeen was racking his brains trying to decide
what he would give her for a birthday present. Her birthday was at
the same time as the great feast of Bealtaine and all the nearby
fairy kingdoms were invited to attend. You can well imagine all
the excitement as everyone in Clonfin began to prepare for the
great event. But to return to Paudeen. He would give her something simple — yes, simple but splendid, and it would be his love
token. He hoped that sometime during the festivities he would see
her alone and then he was going to declare his love for her. He
would tell her all the dreams he had for the two of them and, if
she agreed, they would ask the King that very night for permission

49

to marry. He felt so happy about it all, and he wanted to shout it from the housetops but he must not say anything until he confided with his old friend Conn. He felt sure that Conn would be delighted and perhaps Conn would advise him about the special birthday gift for Finula. Well, the days passed quickly and poor Conn was working day and night making new shoes for nearly everyone. All were going to the feast and the excitement was really great. Every evening Oisin would leave in the little car laden down with new shoes, travelling all over the kingdom and indeed to other kingdoms as well, for was Conn not the best cobbler in all Fairyland? On such an evening Paudeen saw his chance for his talk with Conn. Taking Conn aside after closing the door of the cottage, he said: 'Conn, I have wonderful news for you. No one knows what I am going to tell you. All will know later on but you will know it first. Conn, oh Conn, I am so happy and I want to share my happiness with you! You must know I am in love with Finula. I have never spoken of love to her but now on her birthday at the feast I am going to tell her how much I have loved her ever since the day at the rose tree. I think she loves me too and if we agree then I will ask the King for permission to marry her. I am sure he will agree. And Conn, I want your help in selecting a very special and lovely birthday present for Finula. Oh I'm so happy now that I have told you. Aren't you happy too, Conn?'

Conn, who was seated on his little stool by the bench and was very quiet as Paudeen told of his happiness, looked up at him. What a shock for Paudeen to see tears running down the lined face of his old friend. He had often heard of tears of joy, but there were not tears of joy.

'Conn, my good friend, what have I said to upset you so? Never before have I seen you with tears instead of smiles. Please tell me what is wrong? Are you ill? No of course not! It's something I have said.'

Kneeling down beside the stool, he took Conn's old withered hands in his and said, 'How sorry I am to have upset you! Please tell me what is wrong for I fear that something terrible is on your mind!'

Slowly Conn released one hand and brushed away the tears and then with effort tried to smile, but it was no use.

'Paudeen,' he said in a voice which shook with emotion, 'I have something to tell you, something you must know. Please do not speak until I finish my story. Then you will have to be very brave and very understanding.'

With an icy feeling around his heart Paudeen put his arm around his old friend and then nodded silently for Conn to continue. In a low voice, almost a whisper, Conn said: 'Paudeen, I wished that this day would never come. I hoped as I saw you grow up and watched your love for Finula and her love for you grow with the years. There are many beautiful girls in Fairyland. Any one of them would be happy for you to fall in love with her. Had that happened then I would be so happy for you. Then your wedding would be the greatest ever in Fairyland with joy and merrymaking. You would be accepted for what you are, for who you are. I hoped and wished for that day, but now I know it is not to be. It was always a heartbreak to see your love for one another, knowing that if you did declare your love that you would be lost to one another for all time. You say I am the only one you have told? That gives you a slight, oh so slight, chance that all is not lost. You ask me for advice and that I gladly give. Tell no one what you have told me. Do not declare to Finula your love for her. Do not ask the King for her hand in marriage. Think well over what I say. Finula, I am sure, loves you deeply but she cannot, dare not marry without her father's consent. That is the law and cannot be broken without terrible trouble to those who break it. If you were to ask the King for consent to marry Finula, he would be forced to say to you: To what Royal family do you belong? From what kingdom do you come? You see, in Fairyland Royal families can only marry one another. No matter how poor they are, they must be of Royal blood to marry one another. I know this is hard for you to understand but the law is there. Oh Paudeen, if the King were to ask you, as he must, what would your answer be? In truth you would have to say:

I have no name but what Conn has given me.

I have no home except what Conn has given me.

I have no real name — I do not know where I come from.

In truth I am nobody from nowhere.

As soon as you make such a declaration, you would be banished from Fairyland, forever to roam the world on your own, never to rest, never to have a friend. Such is the law and although the King knows you, respects you and likes you, he must keep the law. You would then be parted from Finula forever!

51

*Paudeen bids Conn farewell.*

'My further advice is that you and you alone must make a choice. First try and forget Finula. Choose one of the beautiful girls, ask her to marry you. Anyone of them would be proud of the honour. You will be accepted by all for what you are. You will have to put Finula from your mind forever and ever.'

Paudeen got up off his knees and walked to the door of the cottage and stood in the open doorway, staring at the star-filled sky. 'Finula,' he said in a broken whisper, 'Finula, how could I love anyone else but you? We were meant for one another from the first day we met. How cruel are the laws that would keep us apart. Everyone knew of our love but everyone was silent. True, no one wished to hurt us. Maybe they thought that all would be right in the end. They were cruel but only to be kind.'

Turning from the door, he whispered to Conn: 'You said I have a choice — one is to declare my love for Finula, only to lose her forever. What is the other choice? Please, Conn, give me your advice, but before you speak remember this, I love Finula. No one else matters. I will never give up hoping — never, never.' And burying his head in his hands, he cried as he had never cried before.

After a while Conn rose from the stool and going over to Paudeen he led him back to the table. Holding Paudeen's hands in his own, Conn began to speak. 'Paudeen, from the first day I saw you, a wee boy, on the road outside the cottage you have been a great comfort to me. The advice I am going to give you could mean that after this night we may never see one another again. It is hard for me to tell you what to do, knowing that if you agree you will leave here and maybe wander the roads of Ireland for a long time. But it is better you go. I will always remember you for what you were. My good wishes go with you. Who you really are or where you come from I do not know although I tried hard to find out for many a long day. To me you were always someone special. I feel that some day I will know I was right.

'Leave here at sunrise. Use your magic shoes, direct them to put you on the path of knowledge that you may find out who you really are and where you come from. Your way may be hard and my wishes go with you, always hoping that some day you will return and claim your Finula. Every leprechaun has a wish for himself. My wish goes to you that I may be able to see such a happy day. I will tell Finula that you had to go away but that you will try to come back. I cannot tell her of your love but I will ask

53

her to wish for you. She loves you and I know she will wait. I believe that this is the road to true happiness. It is as if you are on trial and I feel that you will succeed.'

Paudeen, who had listened in silence, said: 'What you tell me I accept. I have a choice — stay, meet some beautiful girl. No matter how beautiful she is or how much she loves me, I could not return her love. That would make us both unhappy. It would be unfair to her. No, Conn! I was never made feel that my name or where I came from was important. Now I feel that they are the greatest things in life for, without them, I can never hope to win Finula. I would sooner walk the roads of Ireland forever with a hope in my heart than stay here in sorrow and pain. I will go at sunrise. Until then, let us talk about the days we enjoyed together. Let us relive our past happy days since I first met you at the cottage gate. Remembering them will help me in the lonely days ahead. I can mingle memories and dreams and can at least be happy for the days we had together. Yes, let us talk into the night. At sunrise, I will go. I will not say goodbye; someday I will come back.

The two friends sat beside the fire talking, talking, talking, until the first streaks of dawn brightened the sky. As the sun came up over the land, Paudeen stepped out into the road where he met Conn so long ago.

Without a word or a sign he bent and whispered to his magic shoes. Soon he was up and away heading to the path of knowledge. Little did he know then of the many adventures he would go through before his wishes and his dreams came true.

# Finn of the Roads

$A$S PAUDEEN GLIDED ALONG his mind was full of the memories of days gone by and he barely noticed that he had slowly come to rest on a big hill. Sitting there, he thought of Conn and Oisin and Finula and the happy days he spent in Clonfin, and it was quite a while before he realized where he was. As he looked out over the pleasant valley, he could see through tear-dimmed eyes the beauty of spring turning to summer. The green fields, the trees coming to life, the flowers nodding in the warm sun, the hum of the bees, the running brook at the foot of the hill. All was so lovely — so peaceful, yet here he was so unhappy, not knowing what was before him. The more he thought, the more miserable he became. It was too much for him just now, and with his face between his hands, he let the tears flow. How long he sat there he did not know and he was surprised to hear a voice saying, 'What is this I see and hear on this fine sunny day? A fine young man in tears on a day when he should be down in the village preparing for the great feast of Bealtaine!'

On looking up, Paudeen saw a tall thin man and he knew by the quaint clothes that he was a seanchaí or storyteller. 'Let me introduce myself,' said the old man, 'I am Finn, Finn of the Roads, and I am going to the village for the great feast to be given by the King of Croom. But first dry your tears and join me in a mid-day meal. You may tell me — if you wish — of your sorrow and I will listen. If you wish to keep your sorrow to yourself, you may do so, but come let us have a meal and I'm sure you will feel better.' As he moved away Paudeen followed him and soon they were enjoying a meal of bread and honey beside the little brook. The old man chatted and laughed as he ate and it was not long until Paudeen decided to tell him all. Finn listened with great interest and when Paudeen had finished, he asked many questions, all of which Paudeen answered as best he could. Finn sat in silence for

*Finn of the Roads entertaining the guests.*

some time before he spoke again. 'You are a fine young man and from what you have told me, I can see you have a hard journey before you. Be true to your promise and to your love and you will win out in the end. I may be able to help you, but first let us go to the village.'

They reached the village and Finn who seemed to know everyone introduced Paudeen to all. They were given a good meal and shown to the little cottages where they would stay during the days of the feast. Next morning they were up at sunrise and, as Finn went around the village talking to old friends and meeting new ones, Paudeen helped with the decorations. As each day passed more and more visitors arrived and on the morning of the feast the whole valley was thronged with fairies, elves and leprechauns. All day long there was singing and dancing. Music filled the air and laughing groups sat around in the castle lawns or joined in the sports. Paudeen enjoyed himself and for the while forgot his sorrow.

At sunset the King invited the elders to his yearly banquet and céilídhe. Finn was a special guest and he got permission for Paudeen to go with him. When the banquet was over the tables were cleared and the storytelling began. Each storyteller — and there were many of them — told their best stories: some funny; some sad; but all listened to with great respect. When the King rose and called Finn of the Roads to entertain them everyone clapped and cheered. Finn of the Roads was known to all and they looked forward to hearing him. In a short time, Finn had everyone laughing at his funny experiences. He went on to tell them stories of the fairy world outside Croom, of their ways and their customs, their joys and their sorrows. All were thrilled when he told them a story about the Prince of the Rosses and the uninvited guest. When he sat down and whispered to the King, all thought he was finished and they cheered and clapped anew.

However, they became silent again as he rose and said, 'Tonight I am going to finish with a story of a famous island and a famous king. At one time everyone knew the story but with the passage of years it has all been forgotten. Tonight I will tell you about the Isle of Coosanure, about its King, who was also Árd-Rí, and how one night the Island with its King and people vanished without trace and, as far as is known, no one knows why.' He went on to tell them all he knew, having heard the story from other storytellers who in turn had heard it from others long ago. He told them about the Island, the Árd-Rí, the Blue Diamond, and how two days after the great carnival of *Lá an Árd-Rí* the island vanished.

'We must never forget that before Tara of the Kings there was the Isle of Coosanure. When the Island disappeared there was no Árd-Rí for some time and at a great gathering of all the Fairy Kings of Ireland it was decided that they would elect a new Árd-Rí and that his palace would be at Tara.' There was a great silence as Finn went on. 'The mystery of the island did not finish with its disappearance. In my travels I have heard that the Island has been seen on the surface of the lake from time to time. Fairies on the mainland have seen people move about on it and have heard sounds of carnivals. Some have rowed out in boats but no matter how hard they rowed they could never reach the island. Visible one day, gone the next.

'There are stories told of lights seen under the waters and on feast days strange sad music has been heard coming over the lake.' Finn paused for some moments before he went on. 'An even greater mystery happened one evening at sunset. All day long the island was visible and sounds of merriment were heard. Suddenly, the music stopped, the dancing ceased. It would seem that joy was suddenly turned to sorrow for, as the island sank into the waters of the lake, a great wailing cry was heard all over the land. No one knew the reason but it was always spoken of as the crying wind. A great sorrow must have come upon the people of Coosanure but what it was we may never know. I tell you this story so that you in turn will be able to tell others and in that way the story of the Isle will never be forgotten.'

Finn turned and bowed to the King. The story was so strange to most of the elders that instead of clapping and cheering they remained silent for some time. When they did begin to speak it was in little groups and their talk went far into the night.

Paudeen had never heard of the Isle of Coosanure and as he made his way to his cottage he felt that he should know more about it. Next morning he sought out Finn but to his surprise it was Finn who was asking the questions. Once again he had to tell Finn all he knew about himself and thought it strange that Finn was so interested in his age. 'I do not know what age I am. I only know that I have been with Conn for nearly sixteen years.'

Finn held Paudeen's hands in his own and spoke in a strange

*The wise old lady before her cottage.*

way. 'Paudeen, my good friend, you seek the path of knowledge. I want you to go to an old friend of mine. Tell her all you have told me and do whatever she tells you to do. She may be able to help you.' He then told Paudeen where to go. 'Go now and be true to your promise. We will meet again but my good wishes go with you.' At that he turned away and was soon lost to sight.

Paudeen had meant to ask him many questions but it was now too late. Suddenly he remembered that yesterday was Finula's birthday and that he had meant to give her his wish. You see, every fairy has a special wish. It can be used once and once only. The wish must be for someone else, never for the one who makes the wish. Now Paudeen was going to make his wish for Finula. Little did he think that at that moment Finula was making her wish for him. 'My wish goes for Paudeen wherever he is. I wish him happiness and that all his dreams come true.' At the same time Paudeen was saying, 'My wish goes to Finula. I wish her to be really happy and that all her dreams come true.' Although far away from one another both could feel that they were happier for making the wish.

Having said good-bye to his new found friends in the village, Paudeen set out to visit Finn's friend — the wise old lady. When he arrived at the ancient cottage, he found a little old lady seated beside a small table in the garden. When he introduced himself and told her of Finn and explained his mission she looked at him for some time before she spoke. 'You are welcome, Paudeen,' she said. 'If I am to help you, you must do as I say without question. What I have to tell you is for your ears and not for your lips. You must never tell anyone of your visit here or what I have to say. Do you promise?'

'Oh yes,' said Paudeen, 'I give you my word. I will never speak about you or what you tell me.'

The little old lady smiled and said, 'Listen well, Paudeen, for I cannot repeat what I tell you. I want you to leave here and go to a small island on a small lake in the middle kingdom. On the island there is a well. It will be easy to find for there is a low wall around it. Lean over the wall and look into the waters and say, Who am I? Where do I come from? Help me to find the path of knowledge. Keep repeating those words, and if you are honest and true you will receive help. When you hear the birds of the air chatter and you can understand them, then you will know that you are on the right road. Go now, you have a long journey ahead of you. I hope that you will prove worthy of great happiness.' She smiled at Paudeen, then rose and without another word she entered the cottage.

Paudeen waited a short while and as she did not appear again, he rose and left the garden. As he walked down the road he heard a sudden whistling noise from behind. Imagine his surprise when he looked back and found that the cottage and garden had disappeared.

The shock was so great that he had to sit down on a grassy bank wondering if all that had happened was a dream. He thought of what the old lady had said. 'Go to a small island on a small lake in the middle kingdom?' It was all so strange. Bending down, he rubbed his magic shoes saying, 'If what I believe I heard is true please take me to that island.'

Once again he was lifted up and away, far away. He sped to a small island on a small lake. He was so excited that as soon as he came to earth, he ran to the centre of the island and was pleased to see the little stone wall. So it was not a dream after all! Leaning over the wall and looking into the bubbling waters of the well, he kept repeating, 'Who am I? Where do I come from? Please help me.'

It was some time before the surface became calm, and under the clear waters he could see a beautiful castle on a big island. He could see the lovely gardens and so many people. The vision faded quickly and came back again. This time he could see what appeared to be a King and Queen walking through the crowds smiling to all. Running around in front of them was a small boy laughing and playing with other small boys as he passed along. The vision faded again and when it returned, he could see four swans leave a small pond and fly away from the island. The vision faded slowly and the waters began to bubble again. Paudeen was dumbfounded with what he had seen and was about to move away when he saw the waters become clear and calm once more. He saw the beautiful castle standing there in all its glory. Then suddenly from out of the sky a bird — black and white — swooped down and entered one of the windows of the castle. When it came out again, it had a bright shiny object in its beak, and it flew away from the island. As the vision faded Paudeen was amazed to hear a wailing cry which continued until the vision disappeared altogether and the

*Looking down the magic well.*

waters began to bubble up again. He waited, confused and a little frightened by what he had seen and heard, and although he repeated the words time after time nothing happened. The waters just bubbled away. He made his way to the shore of the island and sat there, his mind in a whirl. The more he thought of what he had seen, the more confused he got. He remembered what Finn had said about the Isle of Coosanure and about the wailing cry. If only he had Conn beside him! Conn would understand and help but he was far away. As he sat there, two birds came hopping over the stones, chattering to themselves. He could hardly believe his ears as he realised that he could understand what they were saying.

Said one, 'I'll be sorry to leave here. It was always so safe and peaceful.' Said the other, 'Soon the well will overflow and the island will be no more. Come let us look for another place.' With that they flew away from the island.

Paudeen, remembering what the old lady said about the birds of the air, jumped up and ran back to the well. Another shock was in store for him for he saw the waters rise up over the wall of the well and flood the area around it. Higher and higher went the waters and it suddenly dawned on him that soon the island would be covered. In a panic he rubbed his magic shoes and went speeding away from the island.

On reaching the shore it was as he expected. As he looked across the waters of the lake there was no trace of the island. Now he was more confused than ever and was anxious to get far away. He walked until he was so tired that he could go no further. Once again he gave himself to thinking. All he had seen in the vision at the well convinced him that there was some link between Finn's story and himself. He must find the lake where the Isle of Coosanure once was. He felt that his happiness lay there.

# The Test

A S HE SAT ON THE GRASSY BANK he could hear the sound of children at play. The laughter came nearer and nearer and then he saw a group of little girls coming towards him. When they saw him they stopped and stared without speaking. Paudeen, who loved children, smiled at them and then asked them where they were from. They all looked at him and then turned to one of the group who came forward until she was right beside him. She was a lovely little fairy, dressed in green, with short auburn hair. 'Who are you and where do you come from?' she said and without waiting for Paudeen to reply, she continued. 'I am Princess Deirdre and this is my sister, Princess Ciara' pointing to another beautiful fairy girl with fair hair. 'We come from my father's castle over the hill. The other girls are our friends. Can we help you?'

Paudeen could only smile at this beautiful child who asked questions but did not wait for answers. When he said 'My name is Paudeen,' she asked 'Paudeen what?' When he said 'Just Paudeen!' she said, "Paudeen, Your Highness." I am a princess and must always be addressed as one. My friends here address me as Deirdre because I wish them to do so, but you, a stranger, must address me as Your Highness.'

Pretending to be grave, Paudeen said, 'Your Highness, I am sorry if I have given offence. I am a stranger and I did not know you were a real Princess. If you take me to your father's palace we can talk as we go along.'

The little Princess laughed merrily and said, 'You are very welcome, Paudeen.'

With the two little princesses holding his hands, the group skipped and danced their way over the hill to the palace. On the way he told them a little of his story and then they told him about themselves. Deirdre was seven years old. Ciara was five. They had no brothers. They had a sister, Grainne, who was a great beauty. 'I am sure you will like her and that she will like you. Just

65

*Paudeen meets Princess Deirdre and Princess Ciara.*

you wait and see.

When they reached the palace, Deirdre and Ciara took him by the hands and led him to their father, the King, who was seated on a throne with his Queen on one side and a beautiful girl standing just behind them. He thought this must be the beautiful Grainne and so great was her beauty that he could scarcely take his eyes from her. Then he could hear Deirdre and Ciara. 'Your Majesty, this is Paudeen. We think he is very nice, and we have become great friends. Can he stay for the carnival? I mean for the Princess Grainne's birthday carnival? Oh please say yes. He is so nice!'

The King smiled and rose from the throne. 'I'm sure Princess Grainne would like that and you know that we cannot refuse your request.' He turned to Paudeen. 'You are very welcome to stay as long as you wish.' He then introduced Paudeen to the Queen and then to Grainne. Paudeen was so struck with the beautiful Princess that he could hardly speak and when she smiled her welcome he felt his heart jump with joy. The King then excused himself from the group. He took Paudeen by the arm and led him to his private chamber. When they were seated he spoke to Paudeen in a kind voice.

'You are dressed in white and therefore you are very welcome anywhere you go in Fairyland, and especially welcome here. I may have something to tell you but first you must tell me all about yourself.'

For the third time in a short while Paudeen found himself telling all about himself up to the time he left Clonfin. He did not tell of his meeting with Finn, of the lady at the cottage or his trip to the island as he felt that he was bound to keep his promise to tell no one of what had happened. He told of his love for Finula and why he had to find out who he was and where he came from. When he finished the King said, 'We wish you to stay for the carnival in honour of Grainne's birthday. Rooms will be set aside for you and you may come and go as you please. On the night of the carnival I will have something to ask you and maybe something to tell you. In the meantime enjoy yourself.'

The days passed all too quickly. He got over the pleasant shock he received when he first saw Grainne. Now they were everywhere together and the people in the small kingdom remarked, 'They make a lovely couple. Oh, if we only had him for our Prince and later on for our King how happy we would be!' Even the little

Princesses Deirdre and Ciara were thinking the same thoughts. One day they confided to Paudeen. 'We knew that it would happen. You have fallen in love with one another. We are so happy.'

Because they were so young and so outspoken Paudeen just smiled at them. He had told the King of his love for Finula and he felt sure that by this time all the kingdom knew too.

At last the carnival day arrived and all the kingdom joined in the festivities. Paudeen, now dressed in clothes fit for a Prince, joined with Grainne to open the Carnival Ball. Earlier there had been a great banquet attended by many Princesses and Princes from other kingdoms. The Princes were all in love with Grainne but she had eyes only for Paudeen. Paudeen was so happy that for a while he believed that this was the life he really wanted. He felt that he was born for a life like this. He danced every dance, with one Princess after another and they all fell in love with him. He danced with Deirdre and Ciara and was amused with their chatter. The King and Queen were delighted to see Paudeen and Grainne so happy together, as were all the people who attended the ball — that is all but the Princesses and Princes who were jealous over it all.

When the trumpets sounded that the Ball was over, the King invited Paudeen to his private chamber. 'Later we will join the Queen and the Princess but now we must talk.' He put his arm around Paudeen's shoulders and said, 'Be prepared for a pleasant surprise. I did not know about you until you came here. I do not know who you are but I believe that you are more than just Paudeen. You may never find out who you are and your long journey on the road to knowledge may never come to anything. I will accept you as a Prince with all the rights of a Prince. I have no son, only daughters. Soon I may get the "Blink" for I am getting old. Before I go, I wish that Grainne should marry a Prince who would rule this Kingdom as its King when I go. Grainne loves you as I am sure you love her. Forget the past, think of the future. Your journey to happiness can finish here. You will be very happy and my people who love you too will rejoice that in time you will be their king.'

Paudeen, thinking of his lonely past, his admiration for Grainne and the fact that whether he was a real Prince or not he could be a King of this lovely land, smiled and said, 'How happy I am to know that you would accept me as a Prince and that one day I could be a King. You have all been too kind to me. For that I will be forever grateful.'

The King, thinking that Paudeen would accept his offer, said, 'Come, let us join the others.'

As if in a dream Paudeen followed him from the room. On the way to meet the Queen and Princess Grainne, the King took a small case from his pocket and turning to Paudeen he said, 'My son to be, I have had a special birthday gift made for Princess Grainne. I wish you to give it to her as a token of your love.' Paudeen was getting more and more confused but not so much as to forget another birthday – another Princess – his own love, Princess Finula.

The King seated himself beside the Queen and was about to break the good news that all was settled between Grainne and Paudeen when Paudeen spoke in a hushed voice. 'Your Majesties and you, Princess, I feel bewitched. When I came here I was Paudeen – just Paudeen. Where I came from or who I really am I do not know. You say you accept me as a Prince and that one day I may be King of this lovely land. When I left Clonfin it was because of my love for Princess Finula. I vowed that when I found out who I really was, I would go back to her. If I was a Prince, then I would ask her to be my bride. You have all been so kind to me since I first came. You accept me as a Prince although I have no proof that I am. I admire Princess Grainne but I do not love her. I love Finula and mean to keep the promise I made when I left Clonfin. I would travel the roads of Ireland forever to find out who I really am rather than give up and break my word. Please let me go. My love for Finula would always come between Princess Grainne and I, and we would never be really happy together. Please let me go away.'

The King looked at Paudeen and said, 'Paudeen, is it really your wish that you would forget all this, all I offer you, just for a wish, a dream that may never come true? Tonight I can make you a Prince. Soon you will be a King. Will you throw away such an honour for a dream?'

Once again Paudeen looked at all three in turn and said, 'Such kindness I have never known, such beauty I have never seen before, but it is all so much less than the love and the promise I made for my Princess Finula.' As he spoke those words there was a sudden flash and Paudeen found himself seated once more on the grassy

69

bank where he had first met Deirdre, Ciara and the children. He jumped to his feet so great was the shock and then raced over the hill to where he had seen the palace — but there was no palace. No palace — just green fields. 'What is wrong?' he asked himself. 'I must be bewitched. Finn, the old lady, the island and now the castle, all gone, all vanished. Oh, what am I going to do? What is to become of me?' Just then he heard voices and to his surprise he saw the two birds that flew away from the island before it disappeared. He listened carefully and as they were only a short distance away, he soon understood what they were saying.

Said one, 'Well, he has proved himself true to his promise. Had he accepted he would have gained a lot but would have lost a lot more.' Said the other, 'Yes — now that he has passed this great test he should go to Lough Rí. He has a long way to go but it is there he will find the answer to many things — but he must be there on next midsummer's day.'

With that they flew away and as he sat there he realized more than ever before that he was on the right road to happiness. Now he knew that he was right in putting Finula before everything else; that all that had taken place at the castle was only a temptation. He could have cried with joy for putting Finula before everything and it was with joy in his heart that he bent down and whispered, 'My faithful magic shoes, take me to the shores of Lough Rí and to the joy that is there for asking.' Away he went to what could be his great chance of finding the secret that he dearly wished to solve.

# The End of the Quest

AFTER A LONG JOURNEY Paudeen came to rest on a small hill overlooking the great expanse of water that was Lough Rí or the lake of the King. He made his way down to a fairy village near the shore and was made welcome by the villagers where he made many friends. He told them that he was anxious to know about the lost island. They brought him to a very old man who had seen the island many years before. 'I saw it in the evening and I set out to row over the short distance. No matter how hard I rowed I could never get near to it and when darkness was falling I could row no more. As I was returning to land I heard a loud wailing cry and then to my surprise I saw the island sink into the waters. I was up at dawn but, as I feared, the island was no more. That was sixteen years ago on midsummer's day. I have never seen the island again. Come and I'll show you where I saw it.'

Paudeen followed and was surprised to find that the place pointed out to him was between two headlands dividing the big lake and a smaller inland lake. Paudeen thanked the old man and made a promise that each day at dawn he would look out for a sign from the top of the hill. Well, that is just what he did. As he sat there day after day, many thoughts came to him, many questions came popping up. If and when the island appeared, how could he reach it when so many others failed? If he did get over what was he to do or say? He could not say who he was because he did not know. Who was he then? All he could say was that he arrived at Conn's cottage sixteen years ago, that he was 'the little one' and that he did not know where he came from.

In a flash he remembered that the old villager had said that it was sixteen years ago when he saw the island and on the same evening he heard the wailing cry. What was the cry for? For someone missing? Who was missing that created such sorrow? His mind was racing now with all kinds of thoughts but he was afraid to

*Paudeen and a village boy fix the magpie's wing.*

believe them. One thing was certain, the Isle of Coosanure held the key to his troubles.

The days passed slowly and Paudeen kept vigil every morning at sunrise. The island was said to appear at sunrise and vanish after sunset. For that reason when it did not appear at sunrise, he was free for the day. That gave him time to explore the area. On one such day he heard a bird crying as if in pain. He searched around and around and after a while found a little black and white bird — a magpie — flapping its wings and trying without success to fly away. Paudeen called softly, 'Don't be afraid — I'll help you.' The little bird fluttered and lay still in his hands. Paudeen who loved animals and birds took it to his cottage and soon found out that one of its wings was hurt. With help from another boy, he washed and cleaned the wound and after feeding it they put it in a little box beside the fire.

After a few days it started to hop around and became a great friend with all the boys in the village. Soon it was strong enough to fly and Paudeen took it back to the woods where he found it. Then the excitement started. The baby bird had fallen out of its nest and its parents were frantic when they could not find it. They had searched everywhere in the woods, not knowing that Paudeen had taken care of it. They were overjoyed to have their little one back but they could not tell Paudeen so. As he moved away the birds began chatting to one another. 'We must repay him for his kindness. But what can we give him? We have nothing of value, nothing. But there must be some way.' Paudeen smiled to himself as he heard and understood them but there was no way in which he could tell them how happy he was for them. They were still chattering as he walked away.

There were just six days to go before midsummer's day and Paudeen took up his position on the little hill near to where the island was last seen. Each morning the villagers kept watch with him and when the sun was high in the sky and nothing happened they retired to their homes. Then came midsummer's day. All the villagers, young and old, were there to see the sun rise. There was a hush when the first glimpse of light streaked the morning sky. Brighter and brighter it grew, until at last the sun appeared and the whole lake was bathed in its light. All eyes were now on the narrow channel. The sun rose over the rim of the horizon. It went higher and higher until it shone in all its glory. Higher and higher, but

*The little bird brings him the Blue Diamond on a gold chain.*

nothing happened. No island — nothing.

Paudeen, who felt that this must surely be the day, was deeply disappointed. The villagers too were disappointed and very sorry for this boy who was so loved by all. They moved away slowly and soon there was no one left but Paudeen.

It was near mid-day before he made his way back to the village and remained indoors until late in the evening. The villagers were sorry for him and he did not want to face them yet. As he sat there in his misery he heard a flutter of wings. There before him was the little baby bird that he had helped some weeks before.

The little bird hopped once, then again, and again, and now it was so near that Paudeen could have reached out and touched it. It was then that he could see that the little bird had a gold chain in its beak and hanging from it was a blue stone. He dropped the chain at Paudeen's feet and with a little chirp flew over to join his parents on a small tree not far away, where there was a great chattering. Paudeen did not move and was amazed to hear, 'I hope it will bring him greater luck than it brought the bird who stole it from the castle. Ever since he took it he never had peace of mind. He meant to return it but when he went back the island had disappeared. It has been a long time now. Ever since then, we magpies are supposed to bring bad luck. We hope that it will bring joy to this young man for his kindness to us.' They flew around Paudeen a number of times chattering away happily to one another. Then they flew away.

As if in a dream, Paudeen lifted the gold chain and examined the blue stone. It was not a stone but a beautiful blue diamond. He remembered a story that Finn had told at the King's Palace in Croom. This was not just a diamond — it was the famous Blue Diamond from the Western Isles — the symbol of the authority of the Árd-Rí. Then he thought of the vision at the well, the beautiful castle and the flying bird with the shiny object in its beak. It was all so strange and he now felt that something was going to happen.

He sat there all through the night and at the first streak of light in the eastern sky he made his way to the point. Afraid that he might lose the Blue Diamond he hung the chain around his neck and sat there all alone with his eyes on the narrow channel, waiting and hoping. Midsummer's day had passed. Would he have to wait another year? He just waited and hoped.

The sky brightened and gradually the sun appeared on the rim of the horizon. It grew bigger and bigger and he was so taken with its beauty that it was moments before he saw the island shining in the morning sun. He could hardly believe his eyes. Rooted to the spot, he was unable to move. It was only when he heard first a murmur, then a cheer, that he turned and saw the villagers crowded behind him. Two young boys raced past him towards the boats calling as they ran, 'Come with us, Paudeen. We will row you over.'

Now as excited as they were, Paudeen ran after them and jumped into the bow of the boat. As the boys pulled hard on the oars, the boat sped over the waters towards the island now in full view to all. He had forgotten the Blue Diamond hanging on his chest and did not know that it was shining brightly and could now be seen by the people on the island. What a surprise was in store for them. Paudeen was thrilled that his long vigils were not in vain and that soon he would be able to set foot on the mysterious island. The crowds on the island were crying and laughing at the same time, and when the boat reached the beach there were many hands to help them ashore. 'We are free at last,' they cried. 'Free! Free! Free!' They kept chanting as they embraced the boys but made a cheering passage for Paudeen as they guided him towards the gates of the castle.

Standing there with outstretched hands were the King and Queen and behind them were the elders of the court. The King advanced to Paudeen with tears running down his old and lined face. 'How welcome you are to Coosanure,' he said. 'You have brought with you the Blue Diamond which has caused so much sorrow and pain to us all. Whoever you are, you will always be our nearest and dearest friend.' Paudeen knelt in front of the King. He took the golden chain from around his neck and presented it with the Blue Diamond to the King. 'Your Majesty,' he said, 'I do not know what this Blue Diamond means to you but I'm happy to be the one who brought it back to you and to your people.'

The King embraced him. 'Come with me and we can talk. You can tell me who you are and where you come from. I will tell you all about Coosanure and the spell. Tonight we will have the greatest banquet and the greatest carnival that we ever had, and you will be our honoured guest. First you must rest, for you look very tired. In the evening we will talk and in the meantime you may come and go as you wish.'

During the meal, hurriedly prepared for him, Paudeen recalled the events that led him to the island. It was a long time now since he had left Clonfin, but he still did not know who he was, and that was his real mission. He had to find out who he was. Nothing else mattered in the long run. As he walked around the room, he had a strange feeling that he had been here before. He brushed such a thought from his mind and left the room. He walked slowly through many corridors and coming to an open door he entered the room. It was a bedroom and scattered around were many toys. He picked up one after another and, as he put them down, he had that strange feeling that he had been there before. Hearing foot-steps in the hall he went to the door and called to an old servant who was passing and asked, 'I did not see any boys since I came to the castle and I was wondering whose room this was?'

The old man looked into the room and then at Paudeen. 'This is the room of the little Prince who vanished sixteen years ago. The Queen ordered that this room should never be disturbed. Every day the room is cleaned and the toys left just where he put them before he left. She still hopes that someday he will return. Today thanks to you we are free from the spell and can enjoy the sun-shine, not just for one day but every day. However, their Majesties will always mourn the loss of "the little one".'

Without speaking, Paudeen made his way back to the room where he had the meal. As he sat there he kept thinking of 'the little one'. Was that not what he told Conn at the cottage one day so long ago? He did not know who he was except to say he was 'the little one'. It was Conn who named him Paudeen. Just then he heard loud cheering and, going to the window, he saw crowds. The carnival was getting under way. It reminded him of other carnivals and of course of his Finula. Many thoughts came rushing through his mind but he kept trying to ignore them for he was still afraid that, like other recent events, all would vanish. Deep in thought, he made his way to the castle grounds and so great was the welcome he received that he felt he had to join with the crowds in their happiness. After a while and now feeling a little tired, he made his way through the park and suddenly found himself beside a big pond. He sat on the low bench looking into the waters. Once again he had the strange feeling that he had been here before. Then he remembered the vision in the well — the pond and the four swans.

He was awakened from his thoughts by a servant. 'Will you

come with me please? His Majesty wishes to speak with you.'
Soon he was seated with the King. 'It is better for the moment
that we be alone,' he said. 'You have helped to break the spell
and it is our wish to reward you. As Árd-Rí, now that I have the
authority that goes with the Blue Diamond, I am going to make
you a Prince with the right to take my place when I get the Blink.
I will make the announcement tonight at the banquet. First, let
us talk. I will tell you all about Coosanure and the spell. Then you
can tell me all about yourself.' As the old King told about the
glories of Coosanure, Paudeen listened with care. He heard about
the terrible day when the Blue Diamond vanished and the spell
that caused so much sorrow. He heard of the one day in the sun-
shine every year and of the loss of 'the little one'. 'Her Majesty
believes that some day he will return. For sixteen long years she
has thought of little else. How I wish that her dream would come
true,' the King told him.

Paudeen could see despite the joy of the broken spell, the
sorrow of his lost son on the King's face. At last the King finished
his story and Paudeen began his. He told it step by step from the
day he arrived at Conn's cottage, until he left Clonfin because of
his love for the Princess Finula. 'You tell me that you will make
me a Prince and for that I thank you. But that will not solve my
problem. I must find out who I really am. Even if you make me a
Prince, I am not of Royal Blood and so I cannot, dare not, marry
Finula. Nothing else matters to me. For the sixteen years I lived
with Conn I was happy. Since I found out that I could not declare
my love for Finula, because I did not know who I really was, my
life has been a misery. When I find out who I really am, then I
will know what to do.'

The King was silent as Paudeen told his sad story. Then he
asked: 'You have been with Conn your friend for sixteen years
and you did not know who you were when you arrived at his
cottage?'

'Yes, that is right,' said Paudeen.

The King took Paudeen's hands in his own and spoke slowly
and with emotion. 'Paudeen, I may call you that? Paudeen, you
have given your prized wish to Finula — would you be prepared to
give your next prized gift, your magic shoes, for her sake, for your
own sake and hopefully for mine? I know you prize them greatly
and if you use them in the way I tell you, it may be the last time

they will ever be able to help you, but they may be able to open many secrets dear to you and to me. Think well before you answer!'

'Your Majesty, what you ask is too important to decide lightly. I must have time to think,' said Paudeen. 'They were a gift from Conn and have served me loyally. I could lose them and still not find out who I am. It is a lot to ask. Yes, a lot to ask!'

They sat in silence for quite a while — both with their burden of sorrow, both anxious to help one another. At last Paudeen broke the silence. With a sob in his voice he said, 'Your Majesty, you are old and wise. I have never known a father. Will you now be a father to me and give me your advice? Tell me what I should do. Tell me as you would tell your son that was lost to you. Whatever you say I will do.'

The King was deeply moved by this plea and he paced the room for quite a while before he spoke again. 'I hope that the advice I give you will be for your good. It is the same advice as I would give you if you were my son. Do not be afraid. Ask your magic shoes to bring you back in time — back to midsummer's day, sixteen years ago. Ask your shoes to bring you to the exact spot and allow you repeat the exact words you spoke to someone as the bells were ringing the mid-day hour. Remember now, the exact place and the exact words. That is my advice. Think well before you do anything.' He left the room without looking at Paudeen who, had he looked up, would have seen tears in the King's eyes.

Paudeen sat for a long time before he made his decision. Looking down at his much loved shoes he whispered, 'My good friends, this may be the last time that I will ever ask you to help me. Never before did I want your help as much as I need it now. You have been so loyal to me since Conn gave you to me. I am sure Conn would agree to my request. Please take me to the exact spot I was at mid-day on midsummer's day sixteen years ago. Help me repeat the exact words I spoke on that occasion!'

For a few minutes nothing happened and Paudeen was afraid that what he was asking was for evil and not for good. But he was wrong. Slowly he was raised to his feet and the magic shoes guided him to the door and down a long passage. At the end of the passage was another door leading into a garden. Seated at the table in the centre of the garden were the King and Queen. Paudeen advanced to the table and said in a voice that seemed strange to

*Paudeen returns to the Fairy Isle with the Blue Diamond.*

him, 'Father, may I join you when you walk among the people today? I would like it very much. Please, may I?' When Paudeen finished, the Queen rose from her seat and walked over to him and handed him a sealed roll of paper. She spoke gently with tears in her eyes. 'Open it, little one. Open it and read aloud.' Paudeen broke the seal, opened the scroll and read aloud, 'Father, may I join you when you walk among the people today? I would like it very much. Please may I?' The King rose from the table and joined hands with the Queen. They hugged the surprised Paudeen, saying, 'Welcome home little one. Welcome home. We have waited so long — so long.' Then the tears began to flow, tears of pure joy, tears of happiness that their long lost son had returned; tears that at long last Paudeen had now found his parents, had found who he was and where he came from. At last, he could now go back to Finula and meet again Conn and Oisin and his friends· in Clonfin.

While he was daydreaming, the King was telling his servants to have all the people gather in the castle lawns as he had a special message for them. The music ceased and once again the people gathered on the lawns. What was this message? they asked one another. Has there been some mistake? Are we to have our happiness taken from us once again? It was with anxious eyes that they gazed at the castle doors waiting for the King to appear.

When the King appeared his first thoughts were on the silent crowd. He felt that they were afraid of what he might have to tell them. 'Do not be afraid,' he said, 'I have great news for all — great news indeed.' The crowd, now relieved of the dread of bad news, cheered and cheered without break, and it was a while before he could quieten them. Then he called through the open door. After a few moments the Queen appeared and following her was Paudeen. He was no longer dressed in white and the crowds gasped as they saw he was dressed in the golden clothes of a Prince. As he stood there smiling between the King and the Queen the crowds remained silent.

How can this be? they asked one another. Surely this young man is not going to take the place of 'the little one' so loved by all? They murmured to one another, torn between loyalty to their King and to the breaking of an age old custom to reward the stranger for his great service. A reward, yes; by all means; but to make him a Prince was something they would not, could not

*The King and Queen recognise Paudeen as their son, 'the little one'.*

accept. The King understood their mood. Before anyone could voice displeasure, he spoke: 'I know how you feel but I beg of you to hear me first!' Calling Paudeen forward, the King in a voice that shook with emotion addressed the silent crowd. 'Look not upon a stranger! Look not upon a young man who has helped to break the spell on our island!'

He paused and throwing his arm around Paudeen, he cried out, 'This is no stranger. This is "the little one" lost to us sixteen years ago. This is our long lost son, our son, your Prince. You have joined your Queen and me on our long years of sorrow and pain. Join with us now in our moments of happiness. He is ours. He is yours too!'

A lone voice from the stunned crowd shouted, 'Welcome home little one. Welcome home.' The crowd erupted as one and with tears and laughter they cheered and shouted: 'Welcome, welcome, welcome to our Prince.'

All through the evening and long into the night they danced and sang. For the first time in the long years, they had no fear of the sunset. At sunrise they saw the sun over the lake and they knew that what had happened yesterday and last night was not a dream. The long years of sorrow were over and they had a Prince, their own 'little one' returned home.

# Return to Tara

ON THE FOLLOWING DAY, the King called his advisers and the elders to a meeting in the council room. He reminded them that he was no longer Árd-Rí and that the Blue Diamond should go to the reigning Árd-Rí. They would have to find out where the Árd-Rí held court and bring the Blue Diamond to him. It should go at once and all Fairyland should know that Coosanure was now restored and was a kingdom of its own. 'When I get the Blink, my son will take my place and peace and happiness will reign once more on our island.'

Paudeen, who was present, said that he knew that the Árd-Rí lived at Tara. He had been at the Árd-Rí's palace and was always welcome there. The advisers said that the Prince should go to Tara and that he should go right away. Paudeen who had listened to the debate said 'Tomorrow we must talk again. I want you to leave over the journey to Tara until we discuss it further for I am not happy that we should act so quickly.' All agreed and they retired to meet again next day.

All through the night, Paudeen lay awake thinking about his duty as Prince. He was a Prince and had to act like one. He thought that there was a great danger somewhere and it was not until the dawn that he saw where the danger lay.

He rose and went to the council chambers and searched until he found the paper on which the terms of the spell were written. He read it carefully many times and then satisfied that he knew where the danger lay he went back to bed and slept soundly. After breakfast he went to the King and told him his fears. The King was proud of him and when at the meeting of the advisers and elders he asked that they listen to his son, they knew that something important had come up.

'Your Majesty and friends,' said Paudeen, 'I have given much thought to the journey to Tara. I know that the Blue Diamond should go to Tara but not yet. I have read the terms of the presentation of the Blue Diamond. It said clearly that if the Diamond was stolen, lost, or taken from the island, a great misfortune would fall on the island. I see a terrible danger. If I go to Tara with the diamond, the spell could well take effect again and the island would sink again. Long ago our people came from the Western Isles. Let me go there and see if they will accept us back again. I can tell them that if the diamond goes to Tara we might be lost forever. We can stay in the sun only as long as the Diamond remains here. Yet, it must go to the Árd-Rí or perhaps a greater sorrow may fall on us. It must go to the right owner.'

As he sat down one of the elders rose and addressed the King. 'Your Majesty, you have a true son — a wise Prince. We should do as he says.' The others agreed and the King was proud when they asked the Prince to go to the Western Isles with his plan.

Two days later all was ready for the journey. Paudeen had sent a message to Conn. 'All is well, Conn. Soon I will be back to Clonfin. Have Oisin come to me with the little car. I need it for a special journey, but most of all for the journey to Clonfin, to you, my dear friend, and to my love, Finula.'

Oisin arrived with the little red car and was received as if he were a Prince. He had messages from all at Clonfin and good wishes from Conn who was so anxious to see his Paudeen once more.

Paudeen, with Oisin as his driver, made the long journey to the west. There they got a boat and were soon on the big island. When Paudeen explained his mission they received him with great respect and assured him of a welcome for the people from Coosanure. They were to bring nothing with them. All would be provided and they were to come at once. Paudeen returned without delay and soon the people of the island were on their way to the Western Isles. Paudeen and Oisin remained until all were gone and had arrived safely in their new home. He spent the last day wandering around the island which had once been his home. He would like to have stayed but he knew that was not possible.

He rowed over to the mainland, bringing the Blue Diamond and gold chain with him. He went to the village to say goodbye to his many friends before he made his way to the hill where he had kept vigil for so many days and nights. He remained there all day and all night and all the next day. At sunset he saw his island home sink

86

slowly into the waters of the lake. He knew it would remain there forever.

He waited there all night and as the sun came up over the horizon he took his last look over the lake — the King's lake — which showed no sign of the Isle of Coosanure. He went to Oisin. 'Come Oisin, take me to Tara, then to Clonfin and to the happiness that I have wanted for so long.'

As Paudeen approached Tara he felt very happy indeed. Now he knew who he was and where he came from. Now, as a Prince of Royal Blood, he could ask for Finula's hand in marriage. He could go back to Clonfin and take up where he left off. He was a Prince without a kingdom but he was not worried about that. Still clothed in white but now with fine trimmings, he entered the Árd-Rí's palace. The Árd-Rí welcomed him warmly, saying: 'Welcome, Paudeen. What errand of mercy and for whom do you seek help? Who is in trouble now?' Paudeen smiled as he stood before the Árd-Rí — his friend of many years. 'Your Majesty, I come not to ask but to give! You have always been kind to me and to my appeals for help for myself and others in need. Today I bring you a great gift.' He beckoned to Oisin who brought forward a case, opened it and gave it to Paudeen. Kneeling before the Árd-Rí he took out the chain and the diamond. 'Your Majesty! It is a great honour for me to return the long lost Blue Diamond. It comes with great respect from my father who was sometime King of the Isle of Coosanure. Because of its loss the Isle, its King and its people suffered a great sorrow. The isle is no more. The King, my father, and its people have returned to the Western Isles from which they first came, freed now from the spell and happy to be able to live in the sun once again not just for a day, but for always.'

The Árd-Rí, looking very serious, arose, accepted the gift from Paudeen and put the chain around his neck. Helping Paudeen to his feet he said as if in a whisper, 'This is a great gift, Paudeen, for which your reward shall be great. But come, I must hear more. You were always Paudeen to me and now you tell me that you are a Prince.' He led Paudeen to his private chamber and bade him to be seated. 'You mention your father, the King — King of Coosanure. That means that you are a Prince. One day you are Paudeen from

*The wedding of Paudeen, the Prince of Tara,*
*to Princess Finula of the Kingdom of Tír na Gréine.*

Clonfin who lived with Conn the cobbler — today you say you are a Prince. You must have a story to tell and I want you to tell it to me now. Commoner yesterday — Prince today. I want you to tell me all. I am still your friend, remember.'

As they sat there facing one another, Paudeen told all, everything he knew from the day he met Conn at the cottage, his life at Clonfin, his love for Finula and the reason he left Clonfin. He told of his meeting with Finn the seanchaí and then of his vigil on the shores of Lough Rí, of how he came to have the Blue Diamond. He said that by bringing back the diamond to Coosanure he had broken the spell and told finally of how he found out that he was 'the little one', the lost Prince.

The Árd-Rí was astounded. He asked many questions, all of which Paudeen answered readily. The more he heard the more excited he became and suddenly he jumped up and called for his servant. 'Go prepare a meal for this young man. Tell the elders to meet me at once in the court room. Quickly I say and before you go, see that this young man is not disturbed.' The servant left and the Árd-Rí told Paudeen, 'Do not speak to anyone until I send for you.' Soon after he left the room a meal was put before Paudeen and he sat there for what seemed a long time, all alone. Then, unexpectedly, the door opened and he was asked to come to the great hall. Escorted by officials, he entered the hall and walked slowly through the assembled crowd to where the Árd-Rí and his Queen were seated. As he walked he could see the splendour and the grandeur and marvelled at it all. As he approached the throne he could see a small throne to the right of the Árd-Rí. He wondered who sat there because he knew that the Árd-Rí had no son or heir. One of the officials bade Paudeen be seated in a small chair at the Árd-Rí's feet and asked for silence from the now thronged hall. The Árd-Rí began to speak.

'My loyal subjects, today is a great day, one of the great days in Fairyland. This young man Paudeen, my good friend for many years, was always a champion of what is right and good, was always willing to help those in need or want. He behaved as a Prince even though he did not know that he was one. We will be forever in his debt. He has told me his life story just as I told it to you before I asked him to join us. Because of his wisdom and his love for others, he is now a Prince without a kingdom. The Isle of Coosanure is no more. The King, his father, and the people of the

90

*Paudeen presents the Blue Diamond to the Árd-Rí at Tara.*

island have now returned to the Western Isles and he has brought to us this symbol of authority — the famous Blue Diamond. For the loyalty to his love, the Princess Finula, and for the loyalty he gave to the promise he made to his friend Conn the Cobbler, he has his reward. He can now ask for her hand in marriage. He has proved what he is, a real Prince. We are in his debt for returning this diamond to its rightful owner. I have consulted with the elders. As you know I have no son. Because of his love for others, he has now no kingdom. I have the authority, and the elders have agreed, that we offer to this brave young man the title of Prince of Tara.'

The crowd, having been told of Paudeen's life story, rose as one and shouted with delight, 'Welcome to Tara. You are a Prince of Tara.'

Despite appeals from the Árd-Rí, the crowd kept on shouting 'We have a Prince, an honoured Prince. Long live our Prince.' They roared their approval when the Árd-Rí led the excited Paudeen to the vacant throne on the Árd-Rí's right side. Paudeen was at a loss for words. He could only nod his smiling face at the cheering crowds. When silence was restored the Árd-Rí spoke again. 'I have sent royal messengers to every kingdom in Fairyland inviting all the Kings and Queens, Princes and Princesses, to a great carnival here in Tara next Samhain. Not alone will we have a great carnival but I hope and I am sure that you too hope that it will be the occasion for the wedding of our Prince of Tara to Princess Finula of the Kingdom of Tír na Gréine.'

Paudeen, now overcome with joy, knelt at the Árd-Rí's feet and with tears streaming down his face could only say, 'Your Majesty, I am happy, so happy!' And the crowds chanted, 'A great Prince! A great Prince!'


Well, to finish the story, it was just as the Árd-Rí proclaimed. At the great feast of Samhain all the fairy kingdoms were represented. Paudeen and Finula were married amid great excitement. The people from the Western Isles had pride of place and were joined by Conn the Cobbler, Oisin and the friends from Clonfin. Before the carnival ended there was a big surprise for Paudeen. The assembly of Kings decided that when the Árd-Rí's throne became vacant Paudeen should be their new Árd-Rí and that his lovely

Princess Finula should be their Queen. So ends, for the time being, the story of the little boy whose love for others proved that he was a Prince not only by name but by nature too.